Revenge or Silence

Best wishes

Mark J Exley

Twitter: @MarkEdmondson77
Facebook: Mark J. Edmondson Novelist
Instagram: mark.edmondson77

Revenge or Silence
Copyright © Mark Edmondson, 2022
All rights reserved
The moral rights Mark Edmondson to be identified as
the author of this work in accordance with the
Copyright, Designs and Patents act 1988

For Maggi

Revenge or Silence

A Novella

Mark J. Edmondson

About the Author

Mark J. Edmondson is a businessman from Bolton. He now lives in Atherton, Manchester, with his wife, Maggi and grandson, Joe. As well as writing, Mark likes to read, walk, play and coach football, and is also a lover of animals and nature, and even wild camping.

Also by Mark J. Edmondson

All Alone

1

The light is so bright that the backs of my eyes ache. I'm floating above my tent by at least twenty feet. I can smell the damp smoulder of the deceased campfire as the morning sun creeps up above the trees and sparkles against the dew on the leaves and grass. As I awaken, I wonder why I am floating mid-air above the tent, and not tucked up inside my sleeping bag. The circle of open space in the middle of the Scottish woodland has three tents sited around the fire. All one-man tents, they have their doorways facing each other so we can lie on our stomachs in the openings, telling scary stories, like we always do when we are wild camping. This was something that started in our early twenties, but has continued well into our thirties.

Johnny is definitely the best story teller. His tent is to the right of mine. I have to admit that I struggled to get to sleep because of his story of the woodland killer. It was a tale about a ruthless man-like being that had lived here in the wilds of Scotland, brutally murdering and feeding off the sleeping campers that frequent this particular area that is at least fifteen miles in every direction from any other signs of life. I'm thirty-three now; these stories shouldn't disturb me like they did when we were younger, but this was Johnny's gift. He was talented in many ways, but creepy stories were something that he had a real gift for. I've told him many times he should write stories and send them to publishers, but he always refuses. He loves to tell the stories out loud, but never liked the idea of writing them down. He said it would feel like homework. I was never sure if he prepared the stories beforehand, or whether he just made them up on the spot, or even if he'd stolen them from somewhere. But I'd seen many scary movies, and read many scary books, and if he was stealing them, I hadn't caught him out as yet; not in all the years he'd been spinning these yarns.

The camping trip was a once-a-year thing, but it was in my mind all year round. If ever I was watching a film, or reading a book, I would always have it in the back of my mind that I needed to come up with a story for the next camping trip. If something good came to me, I would write it down and keep the piece of paper in my desk drawer in my office at home. As more things came to me, I would add to the notes. Usually by the time it came to the camping trip, I had a piece of paper full of ideas. I would rewrite them and create a little script for the story. Nothing too elaborate, just the basis of the plot. I would improvise when it was my turn to perform, and usually it would be reasonably good, with a few twists along the way. It seems a lot of work just to tell the story to two people, but as I say, it's something we've been doing for a long time.

Paul's tent is to my left. He's Johnny's younger brother by two years, and always tries his best to tell a story worthy of following his brother's would-be bestsellers. He sometimes gets close to telling a story with as much horror and suspense as Johnny's, but last night he'd failed.

It was OK, but nothing special. It certainly didn't feel as though he'd worked on it all year.

It was Johnny's story that kept me awake. Being alone in a tent in the middle of nowhere after nightfall was frightening enough. The endless noises of all the wildlife going about their night-time routines was usually enough to stop me falling into the land of dreams. I didn't really need a story of a wild man killing, butchering and eating campers to keep me awake. The rustling and twitching of the trees and the gentle breezes that moved the leaves and branches constantly through the night was all I needed to give me a bout of insomnia.

I presumed I must've finally drifted off at some point. I might even be asleep now.

So, why am I floating above the campsite? I really don't understand.

I look down at myself. I am dressed in the white T-shirt and black boxer shorts I'd gone to sleep in. But my body feels strange, almost too warm for this time in the morning. Usually, I would be cold as I step out of my tent, even at this time of year. And the trees are sheltering the campsite from the sun, and will continue to do so for at least another couple of hours.

I do feel very strange though. I'm not really flying; it's more like I am floating in a lifeless way, like a chunk of driftwood making its way along a slow stream. I definitely must've fallen asleep at some point, because if not, I would remember how I ended up where I am now. Surely, I must be dreaming.

Busy shadows from the tall, surrounding fir trees fall across our campsite, as the sun pokes through the branches and leaves.

The late Scottish summer has been kind to us on this trip so far. The impassive and unpredictable weather in this part of the world had tested our durability upon many a previous year, but this time, the weather has been on our side. We didn't waste too much time looking at the weather forecast before heading off into the wilderness. After all, we were going to carry on no matter what. But it's true what they say about Scotland. If you don't like the weather, just wait thirty minutes. But so far, it had been warm and sunny the whole trip.

Last night, we'd taken all our belongings inside our tents before we hit the hay. We didn't think that anybody would steal anything from us this far into the woods, but this was our routine. You could never know when we might get it wrong and lose our essential items. It had never happened before; in fact, we'd never seen another soul in all the previous trips to Scotland once we'd set up camp for the night. We'd seen other campers and walkers throughout the journeys, but once we stopped for the night, we always felt as though we had the forest to ourselves. In fact, it felt as though we had the world to ourselves.

This was the main reason I loved doing these trips. Being miles away from any other human life was an amazing and therapeutic experience. It could be pretty frightening too, but overall, it was exhilarating.

Paul had brought a new toy this year that made us feel a little safer. It was a reel of wire, similar to fishing wire, that he'd circled the site by fastening it to lots of plastic pegs that held it just above the ground. If anyone or anything was to enter our campsite, they would no doubt trip on the wire which would set an alarm off that sat to the side of Paul's tent. Quite a genius invention really. And we know it works, because me and Johnny – to Paul's annoyance – had set it off several times the previous night as we went to relieve ourselves in the woods. It was a high-pitched noise that almost scared us to death every time it happened, so it was a very useful piece of kit. Not that we'd ever had anything enter the camp and attack us in the night in all the previous trips, but I still appreciated Paul's purchase.

Many people who enjoy the pastime of wild camping take their own food and a camping stove. We do bring a small gas camping stove, and some packets of processed camping meals such as chilli con carne, and chicken pasta. But we try our upmost to do the camping trip properly. The meals and the camping stove were in case of emergencies. We prefer to be as authentic as possible, and hunting for our food is the way we've always done it. And we always build a fire. This is against the rules of being a courteous wild camper. You're supposed to leave the site exactly as you find it. But we do always clean up as well as we can. We leave no litter, and we make sure we cover the ground where we'd built the fire as well as possible. Because of our need to camp this way, we have to walk miles away from any towns, villages or farms. The last thing we would want is some landowner turning up and telling us to move on. But we do respect the land, and we're always safe and courteous when embarking on these missions.

Last night, as me and Johnny erected the tents, Paul managed to shoot a rabbit with his pellet gun, and when he'd returned to camp, Johnny skinned, gutted and prepared it before we cooked it in a pan over the campfire.

I've never really liked that part of the trips, and never take part in the gruesome task of preparing the kills. But Johnny and Paul were right really, if we weren't killing and preparing our own food, we'd be eating some other animal that someone else had killed for us. It was just something I didn't particularly enjoy. But it didn't seem to bother Johnny and Paul so I left them to it.

The taste of the rabbit wasn't anything you would re-order on a second trip to a restaurant, but I have to admit, it was the satisfying taste of success and survival that we have become accustomed to over the years. We all find it very rewarding to get back to nature, catching our own food and gathering our own water. Even if I did feel a little guilty at killing these creatures, it just seems like the right thing to do. Johnny sometimes jokes that these are essential skills to have in case your partner ever kicks you out of the house. But really, it's the getting out into the wild that we love. We all have our mobile phones with us, but after walking for a few hours, we rarely have a signal, and in a strange way, this makes us enjoy the experience even more. Peace, quiet, seclusion and tranquillity, and more importantly, the chance to leave the hustle and bustle of everyday life behind. This annual jaunt is something we look forward to all year. And I couldn't ever imagine not going on these trips.

I hear a yawn. It sounds like it's coming from Johnny's tent to my right. There's a rustling noise, followed by the sound of his tent flap unzipping before he clambers out. He's also wearing a white T-shirt, only his has the number seventy-eight printed on it in black. He stumbles towards the trees behind his tent and relieves himself. He then yawns again.

I wait until he's finished before I shout to him; I don't want to scare him mid-flow.

Once he's finished, he walks back to his tent and stretches and groans.

'Up here, Johnny,' I say, softly. He doesn't hear me, so I try again. 'Johnny, I'm up here.'

He seems to look in my direction, but he isn't really looking at me. It's obvious he's just admiring the blue summer's sky through the gaps in the trees.

'Johnny!' I shout.

He doesn't respond, or even flinch. He just turns and heads back into his tent. I suddenly start to get a bad feeling in my stomach.

I try to shift myself, but although I can move all my limbs, I can't move forwards, or backwards. I feel trapped, but I also feel very comfortable, almost like I'm in water that is just the right temperature, neither hot nor cold. I'm just floating and waiting.

Johnny comes out of his tent again. This time he has his brown combat pants and his walking boots on. Although he's the same age as me, and Paul is two years younger at thirty-one, Johnny is the fittest of all of us, which I know only too well when we hike up and down the rough, unforgiving terrain of the Scottish hills. Everything has to be a race with Johnny, whereas I prefer to go at my own pace, and enjoy the experience, and above all, the scenery.

The previous day Paul argued with Johnny that we should slow down, which was the one and only time he has ever sided with me during a disagreement. I knew that in Paul's case, his suggestion of a slower pace was because he was at least three stone overweight, and not because he was enjoying the landscape like I was. But we both wanted Johnny to lighten up a little, and stop making a competition out of everything.

Johnny pulls the small camping stool from his tent, unfolds it, and sits down in front of the fire as he tries to get it going again.

'No,' I shout. 'Go and wake me up.' This sentence wouldn't normally make sense, but at this moment, it kind of does.

He doesn't answer.

I want him to go and wake me up so I can return to earth and get ready for the next part of our journey. As enjoyable as it is to float twenty feet in the air on a sunny August morning, I don't want to stay like this forever.

He pokes at the dead ashes of the fire with a twig and stacks a handful of branches that we'd collected the night before but hadn't used, and carefully places them in the ashes of the previous night's fire. He then takes a roll of toilet paper from inside the door of his tent, takes a good handful, and sets it ablaze by scraping his penknife along the piece of flint as it catches fire within a few strikes. Once he pushes the paper into the centre of the branches, the fire really takes.

Johnny then gets the metal stand and places it over the fire before resting the saucepan on top. On his next trip inside his tent, he fetches the bottle of water and the plastic carrier bag containing the teabags, milk, sugar and three plastic cups.

I have no choice but to float here and watch him while he's busy at work. There's something interesting about watching somebody go about a task when they don't know you're watching them. I'd never realised this before, but I'm finding the simple task of Johnny making a cup of tea – hopefully one for each of us – quite soothing to observe. He is very proficient at the hands-on side of camping and hunting, always taking control of the fire and our kills. I always thought this was amusing, with him being an accountant. It's not that accountants can't do this sort of thing, and I've known Johnny all my life and know how capable he is at doing anything he puts his mind to. But if anyone was watching when he handled any of these woodsman tasks, they would definitely be surprised to find out that he sat behind a desk for a living.

Thankfully, he sets out all three cups. A few moments later, the water is hot enough, and he finishes making the morning drinks.

'Paul! Tom!' he shouts.

I listen.

'Come on; time to get up.'

'OK,' I hear Paul mutter.

I listen for my own voice, but it doesn't come.

I hear Paul yawn and groan. Moments later he makes his way out of his tent.

He stands there, belly overhanging the Superman pyjama bottoms that Johnny had made fun of the previous night.

'Morning,' Johnny says.

'Morning,' Paul replies. 'Is Tom not up yet? He's normally the first one up.' That was true. I don't know why but I always seem to wake up before the others.

'Not this morning,' Johnny says. 'Give him a nudge.'

Paul hobbles over to my tent, still barefoot, and shakes the sides. 'Come on, Tommy. It's morning.'

'I'm up here,' I shout. They don't hear me. I didn't really think they would, but as there was no answer from inside my tent, I thought I would give it a go.

Paul crouches down and grabs hold of the zip to my tent flap. He slowly pulls the zip to the top. 'Hey, Tom, come on, it's time to get up.'

As he pushes the flaps aside, he freezes, just for a few seconds. Then he jumps backwards away from the tent and lands on his backside. 'Shittin' hell!' he shouts.

'What?' Johnny says.

'My God,' Paul shouts, scrambling to his feet. He then runs over to the trees and starts to heave. On the fourth attempt he is finally sick.

'What is it?' Johnny shouts.

Paul is too busy to answer, so Johnny gets to his feet and goes over to my tent to look. As he pulls back the tent flaps, he freezes, just like Paul had. But he doesn't turn to run away and be sick. He just crouches, staring into the tent.

I might be floating twenty feet in the air, but I'm at the wrong angle to see what they can see. I'm hoping that this is some sort of dream, but now it's becoming obvious to me that this isn't the case.

The feeling in my stomach worsens as the scene in front of me seems to have frozen, almost as though someone has pressed the pause button.

Johnny just stares into the tent.

2

I don't know what Johnny can see, but I'm starting to get a good idea. It suddenly comes to me why I am here. I think I know anyway, but I'm hoping I'm wrong. I thought I was dreaming, but I don't think that's what's happening.

I've died.

Even though I'm floating in a strangely comfortable way, the shock of this realisation causes an unbelievable pain in my stomach. I feel scared, sick, nervous. But I also feel as though it can't be happening.

I can't have died, surely. I haven't finished yet. I have more to do, more to see. I haven't had children yet, I haven't seen all the places I want to see. This can't be the end of my life. I feel as though I want to cry, but I can't. There are too many questions running through my mind.

I'm starting to wonder what has caused this to happen.

My first thought is that maybe my heart has packed in. Recently, I haven't felt as strong as I normally do when taking part in activities like hiking. I hadn't been keeping fit like I used to, and alcohol had become part of my daily routine for a while now. Not to any serious amounts, just a couple of cans of lager to help me sleep.

That's it. It's my head. I had a terrible headache a couple of days before coming to Scotland; it could be a brain tumour, or even a stroke. You hear about people being cut down in their prime by such things and now it's happened to me.

Living in Manchester and owning three coffee shops isn't exactly hard physical work, but it can get stressful, especially when people are choosing the faceless corporations instead of paying a couple of pence more per cup to keep a local businessman going. And constantly running around between the shops was a job in itself. As well as ensuring each shop is correctly staffed and stocked of course. I started out as a barista, but recently I felt more like an area manager. And that certainly comes with a level of stress.

Johnny sits on the ground with his head in his hands. I can see him shaking his head slightly from side to side, obviously in disbelief at what he was witnessing. He then slides his hands down his face until he clenches his fingers, almost as if he's about to say a prayer. But the expression on his face is one I've never seen before. And we've been through a lot together over the years. I thought I'd seen every expression he was capable of, but now I know otherwise.

The silence seems to go on forever.

Johnny's eyes seem to widen suddenly, as if a thought just entered his head, a thought he most certainly wasn't happy with.

He slowly stands up and turns around to look at Paul who'd stepped into the centre of the circle, just next to the small fire that is on its way out again. He stares at him, his face suddenly twists with anger. His nostrils flare as his breathing becomes deep and loud.

His fists clench as he suddenly lunges at Paul.

'You bastard!' he shouts, as he grabs Paul by the front of his T-shirt and pushes him backwards until he falls to the ground.

Paul looks scared and confused as his wide-eyed expression locks onto Johnny's face.

'What?' he shouts, struggling to defend himself before finally pushing Johnny off of him.

Johnny is older and fitter, but Paul obviously has strength.

'You think I did this?' he shouts.

'Well, who else could it be?' Johnny says as he gets back on his feet.

It dawns on me that the scene inside the tent isn't the scene I was picturing in my mind. And I certainly haven't died of a heart attack or stroke. This was something much more sinister.

Paul just sits up on the grass and looks up at him. 'It could've been anyone. Someone must've come into the camp and killed him.'

'You really think someone crept into the camp, unzipped Tom's tent, killed him and then left?'

'Well, it wasn't me. I don't know why you would think that.'

Johnny turns around and takes a few steps back towards my tent. The silence carries on for several minutes as they each seem to take in what is happening.

'Hang on,' Paul says, standing up. 'This is an act, isn't it?'

Johnny turns around to look him in the eye. 'What?'

'You killed him, and this is an act to try and convince me that it wasn't you. You've always wanted revenge, ever since he stole Claire from you.'

Johnny throws his arms in the air in disbelief as he turns his back on him and takes a step away.

'That was years ago. We were eighteen years old! That's all in the past.'

'Yes, but him and Claire have stayed together, so you're reminded of it every single day.'

'He's my best friend. I wouldn't kill him. It must've been you that's killed him. You were always jealous of us, always trying to tag along and muscle in on everything we ever do.'

'Even if that was true, it still isn't a motive for killing him.'

'Neither is him stealing my girlfriend. I was happy once I got used to the idea.'

'She was your childhood girlfriend. You were together all through secondary school, and you didn't speak to him for a year and a half after it happened.'

'Yes, but we patched things up. We were best friends, there is no way I would kill him. Christ, we've been friends all our lives.'

'Well, I don't know why you would automatically think it was me. My first thought was that it was someone else.'

'Well if it was, they would have set the alarm off,' Johnny says.

Paul seems to think for a moment. 'Well, it must be you then.'

'I didn't do it, and if it wasn't anyone else, then it must be you. And what about that dying swan act? Making yourself sick, so I believe you.'

'I wasn't acting. I've never seen a dead body before.'

'Well, I didn't kill him!' Johnny shouts.

Paul raises his hands to try and calm him down. 'Look. Let's just stop for a minute.'

Johnny puts his hands on the back of his head as he looks up at the sky. He looks as though he is fighting back tears. After all, he has just lost his best friend, but it also could be the fear of what will happen next.

After a moment of silence, other than the two of them breathing heavily after the heated discussion, Johnny says, 'Is it not possible that someone else did this?'

That's what my first thought was. Why was Johnny so quick to blame Paul? Is it not more likely to be someone else?

Paul seems to think for a second before saying, 'I thought so at first, but the more I think about it, I doubt it. The alarm would've gone off. Unless someone watched us set it up.'

Johnny then says, 'Yeah, that's possible. But at night, it'd be difficult to see that wire. If someone had come into the camp, they would've triggered it, even if they knew it was there.'

'Let's have a look around.'

'Well, before we do, we need to look at Tom,' Johnny says.

'Why?'

'We need to know how he was killed.'

Paul suddenly looks confused. 'He was stabbed. Why don't you know that?'

'I saw the blood, but he could've been shot.'

'The knife if still inside the tent, it's covered in blood.'

I believe Johnny's demeanour. He really didn't know this, unless he's as good at acting as he is at everything else.

Paul knew I was killed with a knife, but Johnny didn't, apparently. But I'm still confused as to why Johnny was so quick to blame Paul. My first thought was that it must've been someone that entered the area while we all slept. But he went straight to blaming his own family.

'Also, if he'd been shot, we would've heard it,' Paul says.

Now I'm suddenly starting to doubt Johnny a little. He is the more intelligent of the two brothers, and the older one and more successful one. Paul is a retail manager for an electronics store – something he's very good at – but his intelligence is nowhere near his older brother's.

I'm wondering if Johnny is pretending not to know what has happened. Although it is possible he's just in a state of shock and didn't see the knife.

Suddenly I feel like a detective from a crime novel, only instead of trying to find the murderer from within a group of strangers, I'm trying to figure out which of my two friends has murdered me in cold blood.

They walk over to the tent. Johnny takes charge and pulls the flaps to one side, tying the small ribbons around them to keep them open.

I want to see inside the tent myself, but I still can't move. I start to make a swimming motion with my arms, while kicking with my legs, but I still can't get any closer to the tent.

I close my eyes and concentrate, almost as though I'm willing the movement. I can't physically do it, so I try to change my location by using my thoughts.

As I open my eyes, I'm annoyed at the fact that I am still in the same place.

I put my hands together and thread my fingers. I close my eyes and try hard to imagine myself standing at the side of Johnny and Paul. I picture the campsite from that angle as I will myself to change position. Though I don't feel any different, I try to make myself believe that this has worked. It isn't so much forcing myself to move, but rather forcing my thoughts in that direction, almost like trying to control a dream.

I slowly open my eyes and to my surprise, I'm standing behind Johnny and Paul. I can't feel the ground, but I am there; it worked. But then I catch a glimpse of the scene from inside the tent. A sickening feeling comes over me.

Until now, I was distracted by the argument, but now it's suddenly hits me that my life is over.

Johnny and Paul crouch down to look inside.

Paul picks up the knife. It's my hunting knife. He holds it with his finger and thumb by the edge of the handle. I call it my Rambo knife. The eight-inch blade is smooth and sharp at one side, the opposite edge serrated for tearing meat.

Paul places it onto the floor of the tent where he'd found it.

As he takes a step back, I'm even more sickened when I get a better look at the scene inside the tent. I'm lying on my back, only covered by the sleeping bag that's pulled down to my waist. My white T-shirt is dark red all over the torso area. The sleeves are still white. My head has fallen to one side and my eyes are shut. My face is as white as my sleeves, but I actually look quite peaceful. There's no fear or pain on my face at all. If it wasn't for the blood and my pale skin, you would guess that I was having a very deep sleep.

'It looks like he's been stabbed through the heart,' Johnny says.

Paul makes a humming noise to show his agreement. 'Stabbed with his own hunting knife.'

A moment of silence passes, then Johnny finally says, 'Right, well I think we should just close the tent.'

'I agree,' Paul says. 'I'll try and phone the police.' He heads towards his own tent.

'What?' Johnny shouts.

'I'll phone the police,' he repeats.

'You can't phone the police.'

Paul looks confused, in fact, so am I.

'Why not?'

'Because we'll end up in prison.'

'One of us will,' Paul says. 'Not me.'

'Look, I haven't killed him.'

'I didn't do it, so I won't be going to prison.'

'Let's just think about it for a moment.'

'No,' Paul says. 'I'm ringing them now.'

Johnny wipes his eyes with his fingers and then concedes, taking a deep breath. 'I suppose you're right.'

Paul goes into his tent and comes out holding his mobile phone.

After briefly looking up at the sky for a moment with his hands on his hips, Johnny goes and sits down on the camping stool where he'd started making a cup of tea earlier. After rubbing his eyes, he continues to make the beverages.

I suppose he's thinking that there's nothing else to do, so he might as well keep the fire going and make them both a drink. They're going to have to wait hours for the police, so I don't see why he shouldn't.

'No signal,' Paul says. 'Where were we when Tom's phone and my phone both received messages at the same time?'

Johnny thinks for a moment. 'We were near that stream. Do you remember? Tom was washing his face in the water when they both beeped.'

'That's it. It's only a mile or so. You make the teas and I'll keep walking until I get a signal.'

'What are you going to say?'

'I'll tell them the truth. We woke up and found him dead.'

'When I've made the drinks, I'll have a wander around to see if there's any signs of anyone else being here. I doubt there was, but I'll check.'

It seems to dawn on him before he'd finished his sentence. 'Wait a minute. If it wasn't you or me that killed him, the killer could still be watching us.'

Paul's face drops. 'Be careful then. Keep your hunting knife at your side.' He then heads off into the woodland in search of a mobile phone signal.

Johnny goes into his tent and rummages around for a minute or so.

He comes back out of the tent, but he doesn't have the knife in his hand. He walks over to my tent and opens the flaps. He pulls them back and crawls inside. He seems to be rummaging through my stuff. He moves my trousers and then looks inside my backpack. I don't know what he's looking for but he doesn't find it. He then exits the tent and goes back over to finish making the teas. Unfortunately, he only prepares two cups. Not that I will be able to drink a cup of tea ever again, but I can definitely smell it. It could just be the power of the mind, but either way, it smells good. I always craved my first cup of tea of the day, but that's the least of my worries right now.

It starts to dawn on me that I'm not going to see Claire again. Until now, I'd been focusing on what was going on and what had happened last night. But the fact of the matter is, I'm dead. No more hiking, no more working, no more eating, no more holding Claire's hand, no more kissing her, no more having sex, no more anything.

It's a strange sensation that's going through my body, but an even stranger feeling that's going through my mind. I'm devastated. I feel like crying, but I can't. I've lost my life, I've lost everything. A lump forms in the back of my throat as I think about Claire. She will be going about her every-day routines, oblivious to the fact that her world has just changed dramatically. At some point today her phone will ring, and her life will never be the same. I can't believe I won't see her again. I want to cry, but I'm too distracted with what's happening, and above all, which one of my friends has done this to me. It could be someone else, but the more I think about it, the more unlikely that is. We're miles from anywhere. And why would that person kill me and not the others. It just doesn't make sense. It has to be Paul or Johnny. But which one of them would do this to me. A tear rolls down my cheek. It surprises me that this can happen. I swipe at it with my hand and look at the wetness of my fingers. Once I realise that I can cry, the thoughts of this devastating situation really begins to hit me, and the tears start to fall like rain. I wasn't ready to die. I had years and years of happiness in front of me. My life was good. I had a business, I have a house, a car, and more importantly, Claire. But now, now it's all over.

3

It's about half an hour later and Paul has returned. Johnny is just sitting on the stool drinking his tea, and apart from the quick rummage he'd had in my tent earlier, he hasn't moved. I keep thinking that he doesn't seem very anxious considering the predicament he's in. He obviously isn't anxious enough to feel the need to pace around the campsite. I know that if it was the other way around, I would be pacing up and down and getting myself worked up. He actually seems quite calm. Could he be calm because he murdered me? Or is he calm because he didn't? And if he didn't murder me, he should be scared at the thought of a killer still being in the woods nearby. Yes, he was upset when they'd found my dead body, devastated even. But there's definitely something about his demeanour that isn't sitting right with me.

'They're on their way,' Paul says, heading over to get the cup of tea that Johnny holds up for him.

'How are they going to get here?'

'I don't know. It took us a long time to get here on foot, so God knows how long it'll take them. They'll have to bring CSI equipment and somehow, they'll have to take his body back.'

'Did they say anything?'

'Yes,' Paul says. 'They said not to touch anything. Not just his tent, but the whole campsite.'

'Really? I've already been back inside Tom's tent.'

It surprises me as he tells Paul this; I thought he was up to something.

'What for?' Paul asks.

'I can't find my hunting knife,' Johnny says.

'Why were you looking in there?'

'I thought that maybe the knife that was used to kill Tom might've been mine.'

'And was it?'

'I don't know. I can't find the other one. Mine and Tom's are the same. We bought them when we were together. So, if that's mine then his has gone, and vice versa. I've checked his tent and the only knife in there is the one covered with blood.'

'It's most likely that the one in his tent is his. So if that's his, then where's yours?'

'I don't know.'

There's a moment's silence.

Paul retrieves a camping stool from inside his tent. He brings it out and sits next to the small fire, opposite his brother.

I'm as confused as them. Well, that's not quite true. One of them knows exactly what happened. But what I'm struggling with is why? Why would one of them kill me? What had I done to deserve this?

'Did you take a look around?' Paul asks.

'Yes. I couldn't see anything. No footsteps or anything.'

Now just a minute. That's a lie. Johnny made himself a cup of tea, he then searched around my tent, briefly walked around the fire, and then he sat on his stool until

Paul returned; only moving to make another cup of tea. Was that enough evidence for me to presume that Johnny was my killer? He didn't check around the campsite and he seemed to be submissive when Paul voiced his ideas earlier, something that I'd never seen in him before. So, did Johnny, my best friend in the whole world, kill me?

I'm also wondering why they aren't doing as they were told. Paul said the police told him not to touch anything within the camp, and yet he's taken a stool from his tent, sat down, and even started drinking a cup of tea. I understand that they've already touched everything. But if there's a possibility that someone else has murdered me, then they shouldn't be sat there.

'While we are waiting,' Johnny says, 'let's discuss motive.'

'Whose?' Paul asks.

'Both of ours.'

Paul looks intrigued. 'Go on then.'

'Right, well, I said before that you were jealous of our friendship. Is that true?'

Being jealous isn't something that people tend to admit to, I'm thinking.

'I'm not jealous,' Paul says. 'Do I have a friendship with anybody as close as yours and Tom's? No, I don't. But that doesn't mean I'm desperate for that. You and Tom might have houses and women in your lives, and you might have kids, but I'm happy in my apartment, living a single man's life. And don't forget, your friendship hasn't always been perfect. Trust me, I'm happy.'

'I didn't say you weren't happy,' Johnny says.

'Don't give me that. I've seen the way you look at me; sometimes all I see from you and Tom is pity in your eyes. I don't need that. I'm doing just fine.'

Johnny bowed his head and took a breath.

'You'd love your own kids though. I've seen the way you are with Lucy and Sally.'

This seemed to annoy Paul a little as he fixed his eyes on Johnny. 'I love them kids, of course, I do, and I'd do anything for them. But that doesn't mean I want my own.'

'OK. What else then?' Johnny says, changing the subject. This obviously isn't an avenue he wants to continue going down.

'Money,' Paul says, folding his arms after putting his cup on the ground.

'What?'

'He lent you money to start your accountancy firm. If Tom is dead, you won't have to pay him back.'

'That's not true. Tom invested in my firm, so we could buy the office instead of renting. But I'll still have to pay Claire. Investments like that pass down to your next of kin. He put up the money to buy the building, so he gets a percentage of the turnover and a monthly sum off the loan for the next nine years. That will continue to his widow.'

I didn't know if that was the case. The dealings are in my name and his, not Claire's. And the fact of the matter is, although Claire and I have been together for most of our adult lives, we've never tied the knot. Which is going to make things very complicated for her, with the house and my shops. But he's the accountant, not me. So maybe he's right. Or maybe he's lying and he does benefit from my death.

'Does he interfere with your business?' Paul asks.

'Not at all, he never even comes to the office now. He's too busy making money with his coffee shops.'

That isn't the case. I have three coffee shops, all run by competent managers and between the three of them, it's worthwhile, but not quite the wage I was taking before I sold my window-fitting firm. I had contracts for three of the major housing companies, and over twenty staff working for me. I made a fortune in that trade and sold the company for a high-end six-figure sum.

Owning the coffee shops is still a challenge, but compared to the building trade, I find it very easy. It's easy because of the good staff behind me and partly because of having the money to invest into the ventures and do it properly. *Harley's Coffee House* is becoming a brand. One branch in Manchester, one in Bolton and one in Bury is just the start. Well, it was the start, until now. Maybe it'll just stay at those three now I'm on my way into my next life. But I don't like the way Johnny spoke just now. There was an air of jealously in his tone. And I'm certainly not making too much money. Being self-employed is like being a boxer – you're only as good as your last fight. And there is a lot of competition in my trade.

Johnny's tone might be because he isn't doing as well as I thought he was. I know he's been struggling building a client list in his accountancy firm. But as far as I know, he isn't struggling financially. If he was, he hasn't told me about it. But I suppose he could've been struggling and kept it to himself. He told me when he'd lost his biggest client a few months back, but he said that losing your best customer can be a good thing for a business, so I didn't think he was too concerned.

'Well, answer me this,' Paul continues, 'and answer me honestly. What have you got to gain by Tom dying?'

Johnny seems to think about this for a long time. He even finishes drinking his tea before he finally answers. 'I can't think of anything. But I can tell you what I've lost, my best friend. A friend who would do anything for me, a friend who has been there for most of my life. I don't know how I'm going to carry on without him. He's been a huge part of my life.'

Paul slumped in his chair before saying, 'I don't know what to say then. All I know is that I didn't kill him, and nobody else is here. And we've got until the police arrive to find out, because they will get to the bottom of it.'

'What makes you so certain?' Johnny asks.

'I've watched loads of detective programmes on the documentary channels. They always suss it out one way or another. And there are only two of us to choose from.'

'Well, hang on a minute,' Johnny says. 'We've talked about my motives but what about yours? What do you have to gain from the loss of Tom?'

'Nothing.'

'Have you ever borrowed money from him?'

'Not that I can remember,' Paul says.

'What kind of answer is that? Have you borrowed money from him or not?'

'I think there's been the odd occasion in the pub when I've been a little short at the end of the night, but I've always paid him back. So, apart from the jealously idea of yours, there isn't a motive for me killing Tom,' Paul says.

Paul is lying.

He has borrowed money from me, quite a lot of money. He has a habit of spending money he hasn't got. And although he has a well-paid job, it doesn't pay well enough to keep him in the life he wants to live. He goes out drinking most nights, and has lots of weekends away, and at least a couple of holidays a year. He confessed to me that he'd fallen into debt and was paying out money for payday loans that were still accumulating as he was hardly paying enough to cover the interest.

I don't mind helping out friends, but when he asked for seven thousand pounds, I told him I'd only lend it to him if he sat down with me so we could go through all his incomes and outgoings. That was a long night, but we came up with a plan and I lent him the money. He set up a standing order to repay me, and so far, he hasn't missed any payments. He did ask me not to tell Johnny, I presumed because of embarrassment. But now I'm wondering if this was his plan all along. He borrowed the money, paid a few months of repayments, patiently waiting for the next camping trip before murdering me in cold blood. It's possible.

'What else then?' Johnny says.

'Nothing. I'm not going to kill Tom because I'm jealous of your friendship,' Paul replies.

After a moment of silence, Johnny says, 'God knows what Dad's gonna do when he finds out.'

Suddenly, it hits me.

Paul does have a motive for killing me. Yes, he's borrowed a lot of money from me, but this is more important than money, to him at least.

I know a secret of his, a big secret. Not a big secret to me, I couldn't care less. But for him, it is a secret that he might possibly kill for. Especially knowing what kind of man his dad is.

4

You can blame technology for Paul's secret being revealed. I know he will. My house is situated between Paul's and Johnny's, so with it being Paul's turn to drive, he collected me on the way. Our yearly adventure of camping and hunting in the wild rotated with two different things. The first was whose turn it was to arrange the trip, not that it needs much arranging. The second was who would drive us there. We drive to Scotland, only stopping once, and that's for breakfast at the services in Cumbria. This is only a third of the way, but we're always ready for it by then. And we always arrange to leave the car somewhere before setting off on foot into the wilds. This year, it was Johnny's turn to arrange the parking. Years ago, he cleverly came up with the idea of paying a pub to leave the car in their car park. This was something that they usually said yes to, knowing full well that we would probably stop for a drink on the way out and on the way in. We could just leave the car at the side of the road. But we all felt much more relaxed about leaving it somewhere safe, and a pub carpark was perfect for that. We also had a snack before we set off, so the landlord of the pub was more than happy to let us park there for three days and three nights.

I was especially looking forward to this trip because it fell on the year when I didn't have to do anything with regards to the arrangements. This was something that happened once every three years, but it was nice to have everything done for you.

So, I kissed Claire goodbye – not knowing at the time it would be the last time I ever kissed her – and walked down my path and threw my very heavy backpack into the boot of Paul's car.

He folded all the seats flat apart from one, so there was plenty of room for all of our camping equipment. The seat in the back was for me once we'd collected Johnny. This was an unspoken ritual of ours; when Paul drove, Johnny sat in the front, with him being Paul's brother. When Johnny drove, I sat in the front, because of my status as Johnny's best friend. Likewise, when I drove, Johnny sat in the front. So maybe this is one example of why Paul would be jealous, only getting to sit in the front if he's actually driving. This might be considered childish, but it is a matter of hierarchy, and whether we admit it or not, we subconsciously decide who's in charge, or who's higher up the chain of command, with these silly little structures.

It was seven thirty in the morning. Paul looked a little more tired than usual. He was wearing his red lumberjack shirt and combat pants, and seemed just as cheerful as he always did.

Although I consider Paul a friend, and a good friend at that, I don't think we would keep in touch if Johnny and I weren't so close. The fact of the matter is, he is my best friend's brother and not really my friend through choice. Yes, we've spent years going on hunting trips together, and many nights in the pub, but it's rarely just the two of us. Although he does always feel comfortable enough to ask me for money. So maybe our friendship does mean more to him than it does to me. We always get on well and we've never had a crossed word, but I think that we both know that if it wasn't for Johnny, we wouldn't ever see each other again. This was another unspoken thing.

It was a bright sunny day as we headed towards Johnny's house, which was about two miles from my place. As Paul fumbled in the compartment next to the steering wheel for his sunglasses, his mobile phone began to ring. The number flashed on the screen with the name Dan above it.

Paul seemed a little flustered as he lifted his bottom off the seat and reached into his trouser pocket, but he couldn't get to it. As he leaned his ample frame further to one side to try and retrieve the phone, the ringing stopped and a very jovial voice came through the car speakers.

'Hi, Paul,' the slightly feminine and very cheerful voice said. 'I just wanted to ring and thank you for a wonderful night before you head off to...'

Paul cut him off by pressing the red phone symbol on the screen. He then retrieved the phone from his pocket before quickly pulling the car over to the side of the road. I saw the screen say *Bluetooth disconnected*. His face was flushed. In fact, he was redder than I'd ever seen him before, and he was always red-faced during the hikes, and when he was full of lager. But now, now he was embarrassed; embarrassed and scared.

He obviously didn't want his 'friend' to call back.

I put my hand on his arm. 'Paul,' I said.

He looked me in the eye.

'It's OK.'

He sat there for what seemed like ages, and I bet it felt even longer for him.

Finally, he spoke. 'It's not what you think.'

I could see his brain firing ideas in all directions, trying to come up with the best lie.

'It's a friend from work. I helped him set up a router.'

'Paul,' I said. 'Just relax. It's obvious what that phone call was because if that was true, you wouldn't have panicked to turn him off.'

'You don't know what you're talking about,' he said, his voice becoming slightly aggressive.

'Paul. It's fine. It's twenty twenty-two. If you're gay, that's OK. I'm happy for you, especially if you've found someone you like.'

'I'm not gay,' he shouted.

'Paul...'

'It's a friend from work,' he snapped.

With that, he pulled the car out into moving traffic and sped towards Johnny's house.

In twenty twenty-two, people shouldn't be scared of being who they are. But I understood Paul being uneasy.

Johnny and Paul's dad was a force of nature. He was a very big, very stern man. Worse than that though, he had an opinion on everything. He certainly wasn't a poster-boy for political correctness. And he was feared throughout the town. Johnny and Paul didn't speak much about him, but I knew they were scared of him, even now they were in their thirties.

He was involved with some kind of gang-related business that none of us had the guts to ever ask about. Although everyone knew this, and knew he wasn't a man to cross, I knew how much he loved his sons. So much so that he insisted on them living a clean life and not getting into the family business so to speak.

Johnny and Paul were both tough, and they both knew how to fight. I'd seen proof of this a few times over the years. They could be short-tempered, and definitely didn't suffer fools. Paul wasn't clever enough to act tough and create an air of menace around him. But when he was pushed, he could certainly look after himself.

Johnny knew how to hold himself in a way that showed people he wasn't to be messed with. He walked with a confidence you wouldn't question. There was definitely a bit of their dad in both of them, but more so with Johnny. And above all, everyone knew who their dad was.

But their dad wanted them to live an honest life, and that's what they did.

Johnny had a gift for numbers, as well as other talents, so that's why he was pushed into accountancy. Paul had a gift for technology and keeping up to date with the latest gadgets, which is why he ended up working in that field. But they were both capable of looking after themselves and could've been useful in their dad's business. But that wasn't what he wanted.

I really understood Paul not wanting his dad to find out about him being gay. He was old-fashioned in his beliefs. Men were men as far as he was concerned. And although I think it's ridiculous these days to hide who you really are, I could see why Paul would hide this from him.

Knowing what their dad was like, I could understand Paul not wanting him to know the truth.

Now, I'm starting to think that Paul might be my killer. It seems extreme to kill me to keep his sexuality a secret, but that doesn't mean it wasn't possible. I'm started to think it could've been Paul. But then again, Johnny's behaviour is still making me think he could be the guilty one.

I'm now more confused than ever.

5

So, I'm dead. I've been stabbed in the middle of the night as I lay in my tent. I've been stabbed with my own hunting knife, although we don't yet know where Johnny's is. It was either Johnny who did it because he's lying about the money I invested in his accountancy firm, and he *will* benefit from my demise; or it was Paul, so he could stay in the closet just a little longer, or maybe because of not wanting to pay the money he owes me. Or there was somebody else in the woods that came into our campsite, in the middle of the night, chose my tent to crawl into, stabbed me, and then left the scene without taking anything, or trying to kill either of the other two, and managing to do it without triggering Paul's alarm.

Not likely.

There is also an added motive for Paul; his jealousy over our friendship. But Johnny also has the additional motive that I stole his girlfriend. It happened many years ago, but he might still be angry about it. Even though we're all friends and stay in touch all the time, it could still hurt him. And he will be reminded of it almost every day, whereas for me, it's all in the past. It was a difficult part of my life, and not a time I would ever wish to go back to. But I see it as history, but maybe Johnny doesn't.

Johnny and I were in the same year at secondary school. We sat together for most subjects, we walked to school together, we walked home together, we played truant together. We were, and had always been, the best of friends.

Claire came into our lives on the first day of our second year of secondary school. She'd moved from a school at the other side of Manchester, so we hadn't seen her before. Aged twelve, we didn't have the same emotions as you have as an adult when you see a beautiful woman, but in many ways, your emotions seem stronger at that age. When I saw her walk into the classroom, I was already sitting down at the desk next to Johnny's, and I swear to God, my heart stopped beating. Understanding a little more now about the human body than I did back then, I know this to be impossible, but back then I was sure it had. One thing's for sure, my breathing definitely stopped.

She was dark-skinned, like she was of Mediterranean origin, something I now know is almost true. Her great grandmother was a quarter Cypriot apparently. Claire's dark curly hair was shoulder length and pushed to one side, and she had a facial expression I can only describe as moody. I couldn't take my eyes off her. But then I felt a nudging sensation coming from an elbow just to my right. I looked at Johnny and saw that he was staring at her and he was as red in the face as I felt I was. I knew at that moment that this wasn't going to end well.

As I look back now, I know that I played the game completely wrong. I talked to her whenever I got the chance. I memorised jokes to try and make her laugh. I let her put her coat in my locker when she lost her key. I made a mental note of the books she read so I could read the same ones and talk to her about them. I also shared my dinner with her one day when she'd lost her dinner money. I thought that I was playing the game correctly, but unbeknown to twelve-year-old me, the way I was behaving cemented me firmly into the 'friend zone.'

I felt as though I was biding my time... for a year or so at least. I wasn't going to be rushed. But then one day after school, she was waiting for me with a coy look on her face. She smiled and brushed her hand through her hair and looked a little nervous. My heart bounced around my chest like an excited puppy. Johnny was at football practice. I'd hurt my ankle the previous week and so decided to give it a miss, so it was just myself and Claire. The scene was set.

She was leaning on the stone wall outside of the main doors when she asked if she could talk to me.

Here it is, I thought. My first romantic experience was about to transpire. I held my breath just as I had when I first laid eyes on her.

'I want to ask you something,' she said.

'Sure,' I said, playing it cool, acting as though girls asked me things all the time and it was no big deal.

'Do you think Johnny would go out with me?'

There it was; the first dagger ever to be thrust into my heart. After all I'd done for her. It was almost as though girls don't like boys who are nice to them and do everything they say. I'd definitely played it wrong, and my best friend Johnny had played a blinder, as they say in the world of football. He'd just sat back, doing enough to get noticed, but playing it cool, and eventually the girl came to him. I was distraught, but I tried my best to hide how I felt. At the end of the day, I wanted to be with Claire, and spend as much time with her as possible. If she wasn't going to be my girlfriend, then I at least wanted to keep her as my friend.

As the years passed, I'd accepted the fact that the girl I was madly in love with was with my best friend. I had girlfriends, but maintained my friendship with Claire all the way through secondary school.

As time went by, I became the person that she came to for advice, or to complain to about Johnny. I wasn't comfortable with that, because after all, Johnny was still my best friend. But Claire always seemed to want me around. She was constantly trying to find girlfriends for me. I didn't really need help with that, I could find my own, but Claire wanted me to be with one of her friends so we moved in the same circle.

Johnny and I were still inseparable, even though he'd been with Claire for the rest of our time at school. He had a talent for managing his time well. He still took part in as many sports as he did before he was with Claire. And he still made time for his friends. And of course, he spent time alone with Claire.

So that was how our childhood gave way to adulthood. But once we'd discovered alcohol, things started to change.

Aged eighteen, I had a blazing row with Johnny outside a nightclub one night because I'd seen him kissing another girl. He didn't see the problem, but Claire was one of my best friends and I didn't like her being treated that way. It was none of my business as far as he was concerned, but I didn't agree. I wasn't prepared to turn a blind eye to Johnny cheating on Claire. I never told her what he'd done. It definitely wasn't my place to do that. But I made sure Johnny knew not to behave that way in front of me again, which thankfully, he didn't.

Later that summer, everything changed.

There were six or seven of us, all having a few drinks at Johnny and Paul's house when their mum and dad were on holiday. As strict as he was, their dad didn't mind us all hanging around there. And we loved it because of how big the house was. And it was the only one I knew of that had a swimming pool. The house wasn't a mansion, but it was big enough for them to have a small swimming pool in an outhouse building in the back garden.

On this particular night, Johnny had too much to drink and passed out, so as usual, me being the nice guy that I was, I walked Claire home. She lived about a mile from Johnny's house, and I'd walked her home several times before, so this was just another ordinary day as far as I was concerned. But as the journey went on, I was soon to realise it wasn't just another ordinary day.

Claire was drunk. Not as drunk as Johnny, but drunk enough to need linking on the way home in case she lost her balance and fell flat on her face. The story so far of myself, Johnny and Claire is probably one that's happened a million times in a million different places, and I bet that at this point in the story, a drunken fumble normally takes place that everyone regrets and causes permanent awkwardness between all of the people involved. But this wasn't the case with us.

Claire, as she stumbled along the pavement in the dark, being propped up by me, her *best male friend* as she used to call me, suddenly released some words that even though they slurred and even though she seemed she was seconds away from passing out, stayed in my head forever.

'I made the wrong choice,' she said.

I said all the right things at this point. I asked her what she was talking about, I even asked her if she meant the choice of alcohol that she'd been drinking, but I knew what she meant.

'I should've chosen you,' she said.

She stopped walking and turned to look me in the eye.

'Don't be silly,' I said. 'You're just drunk. You'll feel differently in the morning.'

'No,' she said softly. 'I won't.' She sat on the nearest garden wall and looked up at me with a glassy look in her eyes as though she was fighting back tears. 'Every day of my life, I regret choosing Johnny. I feel trapped now. He's your best friend and you're mine, but the truth is, I love you, and I always have.'

Eighteen years old is a good age to be told those words for the first time, but the fact that it was my best friend's girlfriend made it both heart-warming and heart-wrenching. I didn't know what to say. At first, I thought that it was drunk talk, but she seemed to sober up a little as she made this revelation.

I took her hands and pulled her up from the wall, put my arm around her, and walked her home. I wanted to kiss her, I couldn't think of anything else, but I couldn't do it. I know now if I'd had more to drink, I would have broken a major rule of friendship. But I'm very happy I didn't and looking back, I don't think that Claire really wanted me to kiss her. Or she too was relieved that it didn't happen. The words she spoke were a betrayal to Johnny, and a kiss would've made things much worse. She understood my friendship with Johnny as much as I did. Telling me she loved me was just something that she had to get off her chest.

I walked her home and we didn't mention it again for three months – the longest three months of my life.

Johnny phoned me at ten thirty on a Thursday night. Aged eighteen, we all still lived at home with our parents. My mum and dad had gone to bed and I was just watching television. Johnny asked to meet me. I sensed something in his voice; he wasn't his usual cheerful self. When I met him outside the church, which was halfway between our two houses, he looked as though he'd been crying. Although it was dark, the reflected orange glow of the street lamp seemed to shine from the glaze of his eyes, even though he wiped them quickly when he saw me making my way up the street.

'What's happened?' I asked.

'She's finished me,' he said.

I didn't know what to say. I wasn't happy about it. Other than the fact that I knew Claire wasn't happy, I was partly hoping they would work things out. But I knew that she couldn't carry on being with someone if she didn't want to be with them. That would feel more like a life-sentence than a relationship.

'Why?' I asked.

'She's told me that she doesn't love me.'

'I don't know what to say. I'm sorry, Johnny.'

'It's not just that,' he said, shaking his head and looking up at the dark sky. 'She's told me that she's in love with someone else.'

At this point I was starting to feel uncomfortable. I knew that it was me, but I had to pretend I didn't know. So, the obvious question was, 'Who?'

He then took a step towards me. It wasn't quite in a threatening way; it was more like he wanted to see my reaction, as though he was looking for guilt.

'I think we both know who it is she's talking about.'

This sentence left a silence that seemed to go on forever. He leaned back against the church-wall and pulled a half-sized bottle of whisky from his coat pocket. I'd never seen him drink whisky before. I watched as he took a swig, then coughed and winced as he threw the cap onto the ground. If he'd discarded the cap then it was obvious that it wasn't needed anymore and he was planning on downing the whole bottle.

I wondered if he was going to make it to college the next day, but I was sure that wasn't on Johnny's mind at that moment. He offered me the bottle. At first, I was going to decline, but then it crossed my mind that if I could down a couple of gulps, it would be less for Johnny to drink, and he might just wake up before noon the next day.

It burned the back of my throat as I took two big swallows. I managed to withhold from coughing, but I had to try hard not to let it show how much it burned. I don't know why. It just seemed like the manly thing to do and act like I drank hard alcohol all the time. But I don't think I fooled Johnny. Do people really enjoy drinking this stuff? I thought.

'Well?' he asked.

'I don't know what you want me to say,' I said, politely, but defensively.

'My girlfriend is in love with you, my best friend, and you've nothing to say.'

'I don't know why you think that. Nothing has ever happened between us. We're just friends, that's all.'

'I knew this was going to happen. I could see it coming a mile off.'

'I don't know what I've done wrong,' I said.

'You two are always together. You're always talking to each other, even when we're all out on the town and there are ten of us, you two still sit together. I've seen the way you look at each other as well; I'm not blind.'

I stood in front of him and looked him in the eye. 'Johnny, listen. I would never do anything to affect our friendship, OK?'

He shook his head and took another gulp of the fiery liquid.

'It's true.'

'Well, why didn't you see this happening?'

'I don't know. I just...'

'Some mate you've turned out to be,' he said, turning and walking away.

I grabbed his arm. 'Hang on,' I said. But before I saw it coming, he'd spun around and punched me in the face. I waved my arms to try to stop from falling, but I'd landed on the cold hard concrete before I could catch my balance.

The side of my face burned, but I couldn't help but feel some satisfaction at the fact that he'd hit me. It almost relieved my guilt a little. A guilt I carried even though I hadn't actually done anything wrong.

He turned and walked away but then stopped ten feet or so from me.

I sat up and felt the warm blood pour from my mouth.

He turned around and came back to me. He grabbed my arms and pulled me up from the ground and embraced me for what seemed like forever. 'I'm sorry,' he whispered in my ear. The whisky smell seemed stronger from his breath than it did from the bottle. 'I didn't ask you here so I could do that.'

I didn't know what to say as the hug continued. I thought that maybe we could work things out, but before he ended the hug, he whispered, 'But we're through.' He then released me, turned away and walked in the direction of his home.

That sentence hurt more than the right-hook he'd just bestowed upon me. That was the last time we spoke for eighteen months.

A lot of water made its way under the bridge within those months. Claire and I got together, which was a dream come true for me, even though I was never happy at how it happened. But I couldn't help how I felt, I loved her. I've loved her ever since I first met her. I don't necessarily believe in love at first sight because you don't know the person at that stage. But I was besotted at first sight, and as I grew to know her, that turned into love. She was the kindest and sweetest girl I'd ever met. And as we grew into our twenties, and now our thirties, our love grew stronger and stronger. We hadn't had children as of yet, but we were planning on having them, one at least. But I guess that won't be happening now.

Once I'd heard that Johnny had met a girl who was to become his future wife, Jenny, I thought that I should try to resolve things with him, especially once I'd found out she was pregnant. He agreed to meet me in the local pub one night. We talked for hours, got everything out in the open and made a fresh start. It was like we'd never been apart. I thought that we were OK from then on, but now, suddenly, I'm not so sure.

As all these memories filter through my mind, I suddenly start to feel emotional again. I'm surprised my emotions have followed me into death. And the more I think about what happened, and the more I think about Claire, all those feelings are coming back to me. I love her more than anything in the world. I love her more than life itself. And now, after all these years together, our journey has come to a sudden end.

I wonder what her reaction will be. I wonder how long it will take her to get over it. Will she meet someone else? Will she get married to them? Will she have children?

This really isn't fair.

I haven't led a perfect life, but I certainly don't deserve to die. And Claire doesn't deserve to lose the love of her life.

Whoever has done this to me needs to pay. Along with the emotion roused by looking back over my life, and the love I'm feeling towards Claire – and still a little towards Johnny if I'm honest – another feeling is creeping into my dead soul.

Anger.

Someone has taken my life away. And I need to know who, and why.

I only hope I get to find out before I head on to my next life. Wherever that might be.

6

They'd sat in silence for about an hour. Two brothers, one most likely a murderer. Surely, it's obvious to the innocent brother that the other one committed the crime, but they are both as unyielding as each other that they didn't do it. Paul was the quickest to suggest phoning the police, but sooner or later, Johnny would've said to do the same. And although Paul phoning the police made him look innocent, maybe he did so because he'd had more time to think about it and knew it was the only option.

I'm still floating near the fire close to the ground as I wait for the police to arrive. I wonder how long it's going to take them. It took the three of us a couple of days on foot to get where we are now, or at least, where Johnny and Paul are now. I'm not really sure where I am. My lifeless carcass is still in my sleeping bag. But how long am I going to be hovering around my two friends? I wonder if I can change my location to somewhere further away. If so, can I go and see Claire? But for the moment, I want to stay with Johnny and Paul, just to see which one of them will let their guard down.

'I wonder if they've told Claire yet,' Johnny says.

Paul looks up at Johnny as he sits hunched over on his camping stool. 'Depends on whether they take my word for it. They might want to see the body first before they tell family and friends.'

'What's Jenny going to say?'

'What? About you being a murderer?'

Johnny grimaces. 'About one of us being killed on a camping trip. And for the last time, it wasn't me.'

'It wasn't me either,' Paul says.

'I'm not going over this again.'

'You don't have to; the police will get to the bottom of it.'

Johnny seems to click on something as he looks over to Paul with a thoughtful expression on his face. 'Hang on a minute. If they can't prove which one of us did it, will they send us both to prison, or will they let us both go free?'

That's a good question, I think.

'Probably send us both down,' Paul says, ever the optimist.

'I can't go to prison. I've got a wife and two kids.'

'Oh! Great, so because I'm single, I should get banged up.'

'I'm not saying that... well actually, if you did it, you should go to prison. But...'

'Well, I didn't.'

A few moments pass without either of them speaking.

Johnny finally says, 'It could be someone else, you know.'

'I really doubt it,' Paul says. 'I thought this before. Even if they could walk in and out of camp without being heard or setting off the alarm, why would they kill one person and not steal anything, or attack either of us?'

'I don't know. But we'd all drank a lot of whisky last night. Maybe we just didn't hear the alarm going off.'

'We drank a bit, but not too much. I'd be very surprised if we slept through the alarm. It makes a deafening noise.'

'True.'

Another hour or so later, as Johnny's preparing yet another cup of tea for them both, they both suddenly stop what they are doing and look at each other.

'What's that?' Johnny says.

'I don't know,' Paul replies.

The humming noise becomes louder and louder, then suddenly, a helicopter appears over the tops of the trees. It's flying high enough not to disturb any of the campsite, but low enough to be deafeningly loud. It shoots straight over the area and then turns around and comes back for a second look. It hovers over the campsite for a few moments, presumably so the people on board can make sure that they have the right place.

Johnny and Paul both wave their arms at the helicopter as it heads off in the opposite direction it came from.

'That was a police helicopter,' Paul says.

'It was.'

'Right, well, we'll see what they have to say.'

'They'll be arresting us both,' Johnny says. 'You think it's been hard so far but our problems are just beginning.'

Twenty minutes later, the team arrive at the scene. There's a woman in a blue suit jacket, white blouse and skirt. She walks into the centre of the campsite with the other people following close behind. She isn't really dressed for hiking through the woods, but at least it's a dry summer's day. She looks about forty, and she walks with a sense of authority. Her perfectly cut shoulder-length brown hair bounces from side to side as she briskly walks through the woodland and into the clearing. She has big brown eyes and high cheekbones, and is wearing very subtle make-up. I'm guessing at this stage, but I'm pretty sure she's a detective, maybe even a detective inspector.

Following closely behind her is a younger man, also in a suit, most likely a detective, then two uniformed officers and two women who drop their bags to the ground and begin to put their white polythene coveralls over their clothes.

'Right,' the woman at the front says in a Scottish accent. 'I'm Detective Inspector Megan Ross, and from this moment onwards you do not speak unless we speak to you. Is that clear?'

Johnny and Paul both nod.

'Your name?' she says, pointing at Paul.

'Paul Hutson.'

'Right, Paul, you get up and go and stand next to that tree and PC Chapman will stay with you.'

Paul quickly walks over to the tree behind his tent, followed by the uniformed officer, who is about six-foot tall and looks as though he's in his in his late twenties.

DI Ross then points at Johnny. She doesn't ask a question, but it's obvious what she wants to know.

'Johnny Hutson,' he says. 'Paul's brother.'

'OK, Johnny. You go and stand next to that tree and PC Calder will go with you. You don't speak to the officers and don't speak to each other. And you don't enter this circle again, OK?'

She barked the orders, but I understand why. This is no ordinary crime scene. It's miles from civilisation, and at this point she doesn't know enough about the situation to make any judgements. She obviously wants to control the scene as best as she can. It isn't like Johnny and Paul can be led to separate cells, so she's just separated them until she knows the full facts, I presume.

'Johnny,' she says. 'What's the victim's name?'

'Tom Harley,' he answers.

'And which tent is the body in?'

He points to my tent. I don't like being referred to as *a body*, but I supposed that's all I am now.

The two women in the white coveralls pull their hoods up over their heads and place white masks over their faces. One is carrying a briefcase, the other, a bigger holdall. They place the bags on the grass about ten feet away from the tent and go over to inspect.

DI Ross then walks around the camp, over to Johnny, followed by the man wearing a suit. 'Right,' she says. 'This is DC Mann. Tell me what happened; quietly, so your brother can't hear.'

DC Mann is short, about five foot six inches, and is stocky, with neatly trimmed stubble.

Johnny takes a deep breath. He looks nervous, but not as nervous as I would be if I was a murder suspect.

DC Mann opens his notebook and stands with his pen at the ready as Johnny starts to speak.

'We went to sleep at around eleven last night, after having a few drinks; we always bring a bottle of whisky with us you see. I woke up first this morning, probably around eight. I started to make a cup of tea for us all. I then shouted to Paul and Tom. Paul got up but Tom didn't, so Paul looked in his tent, and then ran off and threw up against a tree. I then went to look at what had caused him to react that way, and saw that Tom was dead.'

'Had you finished making the cups of tea?' she asks.

A strange question, I think.

'No. I lit the fire and set the water boiling, but that's as far as I got before we found him that way. I finished making them when Paul went to phone the police a little later.'

I realise why she asked this question. She was going to ask him how many cups he'd set out. He would've been stupid to fall for that, but I bet it's difficult to stay fully focused on what you should or shouldn't say to a detective inspector if you've just killed somebody. And asking a question like this might be a good way of her judging Johnny's demeanour.

'I've been told the weapon has been left at the scene.'

'Yes. It's on the floor of the tent, just inside. That's where Tom always kept it.'

'Why would he keep it there?' DI Ross asks.

'We all keep our knives close at hand when we sleep, we usually do anyway. He keeps his just inside the door of the tent. I suppose it's just to feel safe, in case we ever hear anything untoward. It's so we can always find it in the dark.'

He quickly seems to realise that this might not be considered appropriate by the detective and stutters a little.

'Err... we've never used them, and we wouldn't. Just... just to feel safe, that's all.'

The two scenes of crimes officers crouch down in the doorway of the tent. One of them holds a plastic bag open as the other holds the bloodied knife with a gloved finger and thumb, and places it into the bag.

'The strange thing is I can't find my knife. I have the exact same one, but I can't find it. I didn't realise last night so keeping it close to hand mustn't have been in my mind. But we had had a few drinks.'

'Are you sure you've brought it with you?'

'I prepared the kill when we had supper, but I don't know if it was mine or Tom's knife I used. They're both the same knife, you see? I remember getting it ready when I was packing at home, so I'm pretty sure I brought it.'

'What did you have for supper?'

'Paul shot a rabbit with his pellet gun, and I prepared it, but I suppose I could've used Tom's without realising.'

'OK,' she says. 'Stay there, while I speak to your brother.'

She then walks around the camp to get to Paul.

He's leaning on the tree where he was told to stand and pushes himself up and stands erect as the DI approaches him. DC Mann follows, still writing in his notebook as he negotiates his way around the fire.

'Right, Paul,' she says. 'You tell me your side of the story.'

'Well, I heard Johnny shouting that it was time to get up, so I did. Tom wasn't answering, so I looked inside the tent. I saw the blood, and his face was so white, it was obvious he was dead, so I came out and ran over there to be sick.'

'The knife?'

'It was on the floor of the tent where he always keeps it... kept it.'

'OK,' she says. 'Right, stay here and I'll ask you some more questions once the scenes of crime officers have done their job.'

She walks over to the tent. Both SOCOs are inside it by now, so she just stands whispering something to DC Mann, but I can't quite hear.

After a few minutes, one of the SOCOs comes through the doorway of the tent and stands. 'Well,' she says, removing her mask. She looks about fifty, and has red hair poking through the sides of her hood. 'He's been stabbed twice in the chest.'

As she says this, I notice Johnny and Paul glance at each other before staring back at the officer.

'There was a knife in the doorway of the tent, looks as though there's dry blood on it. He's been stabbed once through the heart and once through the right side of his chest. I'm guessing he died pretty quickly because it doesn't look as though a struggle has taken place, he's lying completely flat on his back, almost as if he didn't feel a thing.'

I didn't feel a thing. I was completely unaware of anything until I found myself floating above the campsite.

'There is another knife, but it's missing,' DI Ross says.

'Really?' the SOCO says. 'I'll check inside again.'

As she goes back into the tent, I notice a change in Paul's demeanour. His face is red and he holds his hand over his forehead, rubbing his temples. He glances up at Johnny with a slight expression of disappointment, or maybe even anger, I'm not sure. Does Paul know something that I don't? It's almost as if he's realised something that means Johnny is guilty. But he's already thinking of him as guilty, isn't he? So why does he suddenly look so angry?

I glance over to Johnny. His expression is one I haven't seen before. He doesn't look angry, but the slight fidgeting and sporadic way his eyes are shooting around the scene are telling me that he's suddenly uncomfortable about something. Even more uncomfortable than he should've already been considering what's happening. Johnny is someone who is always cool under pressure, but this situation seems to finally be getting to him.

The SOCO comes back out of the tent. 'There's no other knife in there.'

The second SOCO also climbs out of the tent. 'There's something strange about the wounds,' she says.

'In what way?' DI Ross asks.

'Multiple stab wounds are usually at the same angle, but it isn't the case here. Both entries are pointing slightly inwards towards the centre of the body. Can't be sure until the post mortem, but it's almost as if the killer held a knife in each hand and stabbed the victim with them both at the same time, or maybe changed position before the second blow, but there's no sign of a struggle, he's positioned as if he was sleeping peacefully. Although, unless the killer had a torch, it would've been hard to stab him right through the heart first time. Maybe he adjusted himself before the second thrust. But like I say, we'll know more after the post mortem.'

DI Ross looks confused. But this was sounding like an unusual crime scene. And I really don't remember a thing.

She takes a few steps towards the centre of the campsite.

'Johnny,' she says. 'Are you left-handed or right-handed?'

'Right,' he says.

She turns to Paul. 'And you?'

'Left-handed.'

She then turns back to the SOCO. 'I think that we need to get them back to the station so we can ask more questions.'

'We need to keep them separate though,' DC Mann says. 'Should we take them one at a time?'

'Yes,' DI Ross says. 'We won't all fit in on one trip anyway. PC Calder, you take Johnny first.'

'No!' Paul suddenly shouts.

Everybody stops moving and looks over to him. He's standing next to the tree, looking as flushed as before, but his nervousness seems to have vanished. He stands there and looks into Johnny's eyes before he turns back to DI Ross.

'It was me,' he says. 'I killed him.'

7

The silence seems to go on forever.

Paul has confessed to the murder. Johnny, DI Ross, DC Mann, the SOCOs and the two police constables all stand, staring in amazement.

Paul confessed just before they took Johnny away to the helicopter. But why? Why wait until now? What has changed since the police arrived on the scene? I supposed he could've been concerned for his own safety. Perhaps Johnny might've beaten him up for killing his best friend, and he wanted to wait until the police arrived. Or maybe he realised that he can't keep up the act all the way through a murder trial. Either way, DI Ross has caught her killer, with very little detective work.

I should be angry. In fact, I should be wild with anger. But something isn't quite sitting right with me.

DI Ross takes a few steps towards Paul. 'Say that again,' she says softly.

'I killed him. It was me. You need to let Johnny go. I took his knife from his bag, went into Tom's tent, picked his knife up, and stabbed him with both of them. I threw Johnny's knife into the river when I went to make the phone call.'

'Why did you do that?'

'I wanted to make it look like somebody had crept into the camp and done it, then taken the knife with them, but it wasn't likely for someone to do that without attacking us or stealing anything. And the alarm didn't go off. It was a stupid idea.'

'Alarm?'

'I set up a motion trigger wire around the camp. Just for ease of mind. And that hadn't gone off. I wrapped it up while we were waiting for you.

She nods to PC Chapman to give him the go ahead.

'Paul Hutson, I'm arresting you on the suspicion of murder. You don't have to say anything, but it may harm your defence if you do not mention when questioned something which you later rely on in court. Anything you do say may be given in evidence.'

PC Chapman cuffs him. Throughout the reading of his rights, Johnny and Paul are constantly keeping eye contact with each other. It's as if they're having a conversation without speaking. Paul almost nods to him as he is led away by PC Chapman. It was the tiniest of movements from him, but I'm pretty sure I saw it.

I'm overwhelmed by anger. Has Paul killed me just because I overheard the conversation with the guy who rang him? It's a different world to the one it used to be; why should being gay be such a big deal? Johnny might have taken a little time to get used to it, and yes, his dad is old-fashioned and bad-tempered, but he might not have reacted as badly as Paul thought. So why has he brought my life to an end? Was it just because he was gay and wanted to hide it? Or was it because of the money?

'Right,' DI Ross says. 'Johnny, you still need to come in for questioning and this whole area is a crime scene, so don't touch anything. They are going to take Paul to the station and book him in, and then they will come back for us.'

The two SOCOs, PC Calder and Johnny stay behind, while Paul, DC Mann and PC Chapman head back to the helicopter.

After they've gone, DI Ross goes over to Johnny, who is now sitting on the ground leaning against a tree. He looks deflated. He looks exhausted. Maybe the stress is catching up with him. Or maybe he's as annoyed as I am at his brother taking my life. I'm his best friend. He should be angry. He also should want to get to the bottom of why his brother would do this. But he doesn't look angry. He just looks tired.

DI Ross gestures for PC Calder to leave them as she crouches down to Johnny. I try to move closer to them to listen to their conversation.

'Has he ever been in trouble with the police before?' she asks.

Johnny shakes his head. 'No. I don't know why he's done it. I don't know what he has to gain from Tom dying.'

'Had they fallen out?'

'No. I wondered if he was jealous of Tom being my best friend, but I didn't think he'd kill him because of it.'

'Well, we'll try to get to the bottom of it. Is he married?'

'No. He's single.'

'Is Tom married?'

'Not married, but as good as. She's called Claire. They don't have kids though. I'm married with two daughters.'

'Well, just to be clear, you're still under caution at the moment. Just because he's confessed doesn't mean we'll take his word for it. The scenes of crime officers will give us a better picture once they've finished, and we'll know more after the post mortem. So, until then, you're still a suspect. We'll speak to you properly at the station, but if anything else comes to mind, feel free to give me a shout.'

Johnny nods before bowing his head as he begins to stare at the ground, looking as though he could fall asleep at any moment.

8

An hour passes without much happening. The scenes of crime officers stay busy the whole time, in and around my tent. But apart from the occasional brief conversation with DI Ross, nobody really speaks.

A low humming noise grows in the distance, so DI Ross and Johnny make their way to the area that the helicopter is using as a landing platform.

PC Chapman comes to greet them as they walk towards the noisy machine. I seem to follow them whether I want to or not and before I know it, I am inside the helicopter with Johnny. PC Chapman stays at the scene and DI Ross heads back to the station with Johnny. As the helicopter lifts from the ground and into the air, the noise is deafening.

DI Ross starts to look at her mobile phone. As we head away from the campsite and gather momentum, there's a vibrating noise coming from Johnny's direction. I thought that DI Ross would've taken Johnny's mobile phone from him, but she didn't even ask him if he'd brought it. Maybe this was because Paul had confessed to my murder. Or she might've presumed that because we were so far out in the wilds, there won't be anything interesting on it. But surely they will take it from him once they arrive at the station.

Johnny sits opposite the detective inspector, but one seat over so they aren't directly facing each other. He discreetly pulls his phone from his pocket and opens the message; it's from Jenny. She could've sent the message days before, but it only came through after we've been flying for a few minutes, which possibly covered three or four miles.

I read the message over his shoulder. It reads, *Hope you have a good time, and please be careful. You know how I worry. You left your hunting knife in our bedroom, but I'm guessing it's not important if Tom's got his. I only noticed it after you'd been gone for a couple of hours. Kids had a great time at the trampoline place. I'll send you the videos. Have fun, love you lots, see you Monday, xxx.*

Straight away, he deletes the message.

It takes me a few seconds, but then it hits me. I suddenly know how I was killed, and I know why. It was right in front of me the whole time. The way they were both being careful of what they said, the way they were shocked but not as shocked as they should've been, and the way they were angry with each other, but not as angry as they should've been considering the severity of the situation. And also, their lack of fear that it could've been someone else. It's now obvious to me.

They both did it.

Once the fear of Johnny's ghost story had worn off, and as I slept in my sleeping bag, under the influence of the best sleeping medication you can buy, whisky, one of them, let's say Johnny, sneaked out of his tent, crept over to mine, maybe using the light from his phone to see. He then carefully unzipped my tent flap, took hold of my hunting knife with his right hand, and brought it down hard into my heart. The more I think about it, it would've been Johnny first because he was right-handed, and I died instantly. Then, later in the night, Paul crept from his tent, came over to mine, opened the flap as Johnny did, and took the already bloodied knife in his left hand, and stabbed me in the right side of my chest.

They both thought they'd killed me, but when Paul stabbed me, unbeknown to him, I was already dead.

Paul confessed to the murder after they'd both heard the SOCO say that there were two stab wounds, and then he lied about throwing the knife into the river. They both clicked on what had happened, and Paul decided to take a bullet for Johnny, probably because Johnny has a wife and two kids, and Paul will do anything for Johnny's daughters. He loves them dearly.

Or maybe it was because Johnny is more successful. Maybe Paul's wanting a payout from him when he's released from prison. But either way, they are both guilty and although I thought of them both as my friends, they should both be imprisoned. I'm sure that the police will get the truth from them. They can't keep a lie like this to themselves; can they? And surely the bleeding from the second wound will show that I was already dead? It must look different to the first wound. That must come to light in my post mortem. *My post mortem...* another phrase never used before, but one that makes perfect sense now.

As the helicopter takes my best friend and DI Ross to the police station, I try to change my location to go and see Claire one more time. The love of my life, the love of

Johnny's youth. I have to wonder where we would all be now if I'd have stayed clear of her, and had given them the space to make their own way. Or what would've happened if I'd had the guts to tell her how I felt before she fell for Johnny.

The truth of the matter is that one way or another I am dead because of love. I'd fallen in love with my best friend's girlfriend and spent fifteen years living a blissfully happy life with Claire. I have to ask myself, was it worth it? When I picture her soft, dark skin, her beautiful eyes and her breathtaking smile, I know it *was* worth it; and given the chance to live again, I probably wouldn't change a thing.

So this is the end of my time on earth. I don't know what is about to happen to me. Is there a heaven? Is there an afterlife? Do we get to start again, and try and do better the second time around? If that's the case then maybe I should look away on the day that Claire walks into my classroom. Maybe I should refrain from being her friend. But when I picture her face, I know that even if I did get a second chance, I wouldn't be able to walk away from her.

I hope that one day we can be reunited. And maybe even be reunited with Johnny and Paul, but only so I could tell them what I think of them.

I feel very strange as I begin to move into my next chapter. I should be angrier, but I feel that emotion fade; I should be more upset than I actually am, but that too seems to deplete, almost as though death has removed these feelings from me. But it hasn't removed how I feel about Claire. Love must be stronger than life itself. And I really hope I get to see her again. Not for a while, but one day. Hopefully.

THE END

Acknowledgments

This is the first novella I've released, but certainly not the first I've written. The truth of the matter is, I never know how long a story is going to be. I've written stories I thought would make a nice short story, but as I delve into the world I create, I usually find that the story is going to be anything but short.

Revenge or Silence started as a short story. But as I worked my way through, it became apparent that it was going to be at least a novelette, and sure enough, by the time I typed the words 'The End', it's a novella.

I've come to realise that I have little say about the length of a story. I occasionally feel that way about the plot too. And I've lost count of the times I've been surprised at the way a character has behaved, or the things they've said. I don't feel as though I'm creating these stories, it's more like I'm the medium, channelling them and passing them onto you, the reader. But as long as they keep coming to me, that's fine with me.

I'd like to thank all my family and friends for your continuing support, especially Bea Green and Angela Sharpe for your help with this book. And also, my editor, Marie Campbell for her amazing skills in polishing my manuscripts. And most importantly, my readers. Thank you for your interest, your commitment, and your nice messages and reviews. You make it all worthwhile.

Also by Mark J. Edmondson
All Alone

Oliver

1

Saturday 1st May

Whitford had everything every other town had; a church, a primary school, a secondary school, a bus and train station, a library, and a retail park that had suddenly appeared as if by magic several years earlier. There was an industrial park on the outskirts with several factories where most of the town worked; those who didn't commute to Manchester to make a living. But the industrial park was hidden away, only accessed by a long road leading off the carriageway where if you blinked you missed it. So the town still appeared scenic to anyone passing through, with all the huge industrial buildings out of view.

Apart from the council estate on the east side which was mainly flats and bungalows, most of the town had semi-detached houses with front gardens and low bricked walls. The more expensive houses were situated on the main road that led through the town. These houses were only affordable to the likes of doctors, politicians and professional footballers. Because of this 'millionaires' row', as people referred to it, Whitford had a reputation of being a more sought-after area. Even though there were only twelve houses that fit that description, the rest all being more affordable family homes, and just one or two in between.

The population was around eight thousand, which didn't quite mean that everyone knew everyone, but it seemed as though most of the people who lived there were all connected one way or another, either by their kids going to the same school, or by working in the factories or the stores at the retail park.

There was some truth in the fact that it was a close-knit community. The church was still a regular meeting place for many, although numbers in the congregation had dwindled over the years. And the local football and cricket teams were another way of everyone coming together, gathering for the weekly games, standing on the side-lines and catching up on the local gossip. And the players from the older teams would of course go for a drink in one of the two pubs in the town, or the bar at the cricket ground, or even the small public house at the bowling club. There was always something going on. If not a sports event, there would be a spring fair, or a bring and buy sale at the community hall. Whitford was too big to be referred to as a village, but there was certainly a village feel to the place.

Oliver Derwent, aged ten, lived in Whitford with his mum. He was drawing a picture at the desk in his bedroom with the charcoal pencils his mum had bought him the previous week. The picture was of the tractor he could see in the distance through the window. It was parked in the field behind the farmhouse further along the lane. It was quite a way from where he was, but he could just about see it well enough to draw a reasonably accurate picture.

The sun shone through the window creating a diagonal shadow across the page. This didn't bother him, or distract him. He was enjoying the warmth on his right forearm as he gently moved the pencil over the paper. His left arm felt a little cooler as it rested in the shade.

He could hear his mum pacing around the house, getting ready to go out shopping, but despite that, and the chirping noises from the birds speaking to each other in their own language as they did every morning outside his window, Oliver was fully focused on his drawing. He always preferred to draw in pencil or charcoal. His teacher, Mrs Wheaton, was always telling him to add some colour to his work, saying things like, *'That would look nice if it was a little brighter,'* or *'Why don't you at least colour the sky in blue?'.* But he had no intentions of doing so. He liked his drawings just the way they were. All the shades of black and grey would allow him to tell the story just fine. He didn't need colour. And he couldn't imagine ever changing the way he created his works of art. He didn't draw for other people's approval. He drew for himself and himself alone. Although it did make him a little happier when his mum said she liked them. But even if she didn't say anything about his pictures, he would still continue to draw. This was how he liked to spend most of his time; in fact, almost all of his time. He would stop to eat, or drink, or watch the occasional cartoon on television, but other than that, drawing was what he loved to do.

Over the last couple of years, his mum had been asked to go into school because of the drawings Oliver had created. She'd had to go in at least five or six times.

Oliver didn't understand what the problem was. People sometimes die, so why couldn't he draw a picture of a dead person? And the drawing of the graveyard was his best work yet. He'd spent hours getting the shading just right on that one, just for Mrs Wheaton to phone his mum again, asking her to go into school for another meeting.

He really didn't understand. And he really didn't know what there was to discuss. He just enjoyed drawing, and he drew whatever he wanted. He didn't care if the drawings weren't to other people's taste, he just had to do it. Once he'd seen something he wanted to draw, whether it was something real in front of him, or something that had jumped into his mind's eye, he couldn't not draw it. It was like an itch he had to scratch and it wouldn't go away until he'd seen it on paper. It didn't bother him too much if it didn't turn out how he'd wanted, or how he'd imagined it to be. He just had to see the finished product in front of him before he could relax and move on to the next project. If a thought or an idea popped into his head while he was at school, he would think about it all day and run home as fast as he could once the school day had ended. Unless he was lucky enough to have had one of these images climb into his brain on a day when there was an art lesson. If that was the case, he would work on the drawing at school until it was finished. Even if it meant him missing his breaktime. And he'd much rather stay inside and draw than run around outside with the other kids. He preferred the gentle sound of the pencil sliding across the paper to the annoying noise of the other kids all running around, screaming and shouting.

Oliver lived in a bungalow next to Hunter's Farm. It felt like they were living in the countryside to him and his mum. It was surrounded by fields, and there was a small forest at the back that led through to the town centre via a nature trail that passed the pond everyone called *the bucket*. Oliver didn't know why it was called that, and he didn't know if it was its real name or just a nickname the locals gave it. And it was certainly bigger than a bucket. It was a little bigger than the large swimming pool he went to in the town with school.

He used to like going to the bucket, feeding the ducks while he sat on one of the benches next to the water, or maybe having a picnic on the grass. But this was something he hadn't done for a long time. Not since his dad had left.

Oliver briefly glanced up from his picture as his mum walked into the room. She was dressed in her red skirt and white blouse, her hair and make-up as perfect as ever. She would always spend a lot of time getting ready, and she always looked nice by the time she left the house. But Oliver didn't like it when she wore skirts like that one. Whenever she dressed in her more colourful clothes, people would stare; usually men, but he'd sometimes see other women looking her up and down with a disapproving expression on their faces. Occasionally men would shout things or whistle. His mum didn't seem to like it. She would always tut or shake her head while walking away. But she still dressed that way. Her clothes were always bright and colourful.

He felt as though this always gave her unwanted attention of some sort. Oliver really didn't like it when people would do this to her. He'd thought on many occasions about telling them off. But he didn't think they would listen to him.

Maybe when he was older, he could tell them to cut it out, and maybe they would listen. After all, they had no right treating his mum that way.

'OK, sweetheart, I'm off to the supermarket. Are you sure you don't want to come?' she said, standing at the side of him with her hand on his shoulder.

'I'll stay,' he said, still drawing.

His mum leaned over and kissed him on the top of his head before looking at the picture. 'That's nice, Ollie. You like the charcoal pencils then?'

He nodded as he carried on shading.

The smell of his mum's perfume was overpowering. He wanted to cough, but he fought it, not wanting to offend her like he did a few weeks earlier. The smell was very nice, but whenever she'd only just sprayed it, it would always smell much stronger, and it would tickle the back of his throat. He could still smell it on her when she'd arrive back from her shopping trip, but by then it wouldn't be as strong.

'You're not going to...'

Oliver interrupted by sticking the pencil into the noisy electric pencil sharpener that was fastened to his desk.

His mum started again. 'You're not going to draw a dead body under the tractor, are you?'

Oliver shook his head before pointing to the tractor outside.

His mum leaned over him to look into the distance. 'Excellent. It's very good,' she said, looking back at the half-finished picture.

'Thanks.'

'You're getting better and better. One day you'll be a famous artist.'

After a brief silence as she watched him draw, she said, 'See, if you had a games console, that would distract you and you wouldn't be as good.'

Oliver had asked for a games console for the last two Christmases and birthdays. He knew they were expensive, and he knew this was something his mum couldn't afford. But everyone else had one, so he thought he should have one too. He did have one a few years ago that stopped working, but he'd heard they'd changed a bit since then.

Deep down, he wondered if he did actually want something like that. Just because it was all everyone ever talked about at school didn't mean it would be something he would enjoy.

Drawing was his passion, and he didn't really want anything to get in the way of that. And the games console he had when his dad still lived with them – as great as it was to play with another person like his mum or dad – he found that he became bored of it when playing on his own. He knew the new consoles would've been much better by now, even though it was only a few years ago. But he still wasn't sure it was what he wanted. Asking for one just felt like the right thing to do. He wondered if he should tell his mum he wasn't that bothered, just in case she was putting money aside, trying to save up. That money would be better used on other things, like decent food instead of the cheap stuff she would normally buy. And she'd talked about needing new windows for the bungalow before now. He didn't know what was wrong with the ones they had. Although he had noticed the wood crumbling a little on the outside frame of his bedroom.

From the corner of his eye, he watched his mum pick up the unopened pack of coloured pencils from his desk. 'I see these were a waste of money,' she said.

He smiled and carried on with his shading.

'Right, I'm going. Is there anything you want?' she said as she walked away.

'Chocolate,' he said.

'I know that,' she answered, then turned back to him. 'You be good.'

'OK.'

'I'll be back in twenty minutes,' she said as she left the room.

'Mum!' Oliver shouted.

She poked her head around the door.

'I heard voices this morning.'

She suddenly looked a little flustered, as though he'd asked her something he shouldn't. 'Voices?'

'Yes. It was really early. The sun was up, but I think it was only about six o'clock. It sounded like a man talking.'

'Oh... err... that was just the television. I fell asleep on the sofa last night so the TV was still on when I woke up.'

'OK,' Oliver said.

After a moment's silence, she said, 'Twenty minutes, OK?', smiling once more.

Shortly after, he heard his mum go through the door in the kitchen that led to outside, and then she locked it. Oliver then heard the car making its usual grinding sounds before it finally started. It then fell quieter and quieter as his mum drove the car down the lane until he could no longer hear it.

The bungalow was on the outskirts of Whitford. It was a long way from anywhere else in the town as it was built on the land of Hunter's Farm. It stood at the bottom of the long and dusty gravel road that led from the carriageway. The farmhouse was about fifty metres away. Oliver occasionally had to walk past the farm to go to school, usually when his mum's car wasn't working.

He didn't like the farm. Mostly because of the huge German Shepherd who went by the name of Kaiser; Oliver was terrified of him. Kaiser was mostly black with the odd patch of brown on his chest. He always had a trail of spit hanging from the corners of his mouth, and he had one white eye. Oliver didn't know if he'd been injured at some point in his life or if he was born that way. But he looked all the more menacing for it; a menacing image Oliver had seen in many of his nightmares. He was a vicious dog, and he would run at Oliver barking and snarling whenever he walked by. He hadn't bitten him as of yet because the farmer would always shout him back before he did. But Oliver always wondered what would happen if the farmer wasn't there one day. Was Kaiser's bark worse than his bite? Or would he sink his teeth into the back of his neck as he tried to run away?

Oliver didn't like the farmer much either. His name was Len Hunter, and he was horrible. He was a bit younger than his mum, and he was thin and pale with messy hair. Oliver especially didn't like his eyes. He didn't know what it was about them, but they looked evil to him. He also looked at Oliver's mum in the way he didn't like, just like all the other men did; only worse. Mr Hunter would put his hands on his hips and make a groaning sound as he looked her up and down. Oliver didn't like people doing that. He understood that his mum was pretty. She had long dark, wavy hair, and he'd heard people say she had curves to die for, whatever that meant. Usually, it was a woman who would say that to her, which his mum didn't seem to mind. But it was when men stared at her that she wasn't happy, and neither was Oliver. Which is why he didn't want to go to the supermarket. He'd rather stay at home and draw.

He looked at the clock on his bedroom wall. This was something he did often, especially when his mum had gone out. He didn't mind being left alone, but he was always a little anxious. He was much happier when she was home. The clock read thirteen minutes past eleven, so if his mum was back within twenty minutes, then she should be home by eleven thirty-three, he thought. But he knew she wouldn't be. It was going to be at least an hour. It always was.

2

'Finished,' Oliver said, the sound of his own voice breaking the deathly silence of the room.

He pulled some pieces of sticky-tape off the roll, cutting each piece by pulling it against the serrated metal edge of the holder, and then carefully placed them in each corner of the paper. Once he'd made his way across the bedroom, he climbed onto his bed, and stuck it to the wall with all the others. There was a space between the picture of Kaiser – which, he admitted to his mum, didn't look much like him – and the picture of a ghostly figure he'd drawn making its way along one of the school corridors. He'd created that picture while at school and it had caused another spot of bother. The head teacher, Mr Grimes, had walked into the classroom to talk to Mrs Wheaton. He stopped talking to her when he saw Oliver's artwork, and told him how much he liked it. But when he noticed the faint outline of the figure of a man dressed in baggy robes, looking like the Grim Reaper – except carrying a wooden staff instead of a scythe – the compliments suddenly stopped and he and Mrs Wheaton walked away and had a private discussion. His mum was called into school yet again.

Oliver looked at the clock on his bedroom wall, on the opposite side to all his pictures. It was eleven forty-five. She was already twelve minutes late. He rolled his eyes and wandered through to the kitchen. Once there, he took a chair out from under the kitchen table, dragged it over to the cupboards and climbed onto it so he could reach the snacks.

He took out a couple of chocolate bars, then closed the cupboard door before putting the chair back. As long as he put the wrappers in the bin and pushed them down a little, his mum wouldn't know he'd eaten two. It was the perfect crime.

He ate in front of the television as he watched cartoons. Although he didn't like being left alone for too long, he hoped his mum would be out longer than usual. If she started making dinner as soon as she got back, he knew he wouldn't be able to finish the meal, not after eating two chocolate bars. But if she was another half an hour or so, he thought there would be more chance of him managing to eat it all.

She didn't like it when he wasted food. And he understood why. Money was tight and it was a waste for her to buy and cook food for him just for it to end up in the bin, as she'd told him many times before.

It was always about this time on a Saturday when his dad would get out of bed. He'd worked hard all week, so on Saturdays he would sleep in until dinner, and on Sundays he would get up earlier to work on the house or the garden, or to take Oliver and his mum out somewhere.

It was almost two years since his dad left without saying goodbye. Oliver was only eight at the time. He was very sad when he'd first left, but not nearly as sad as his mum was. She'd cried and cried every night for weeks. Oliver cried too, but as much as he missed his dad, and was upset that he'd gone, he only ever cried when he saw his mum crying. There was something about how sad she looked and the expression on her face that caused him to shed tears too. He still missed his dad, and hoped he would come back one day. Even now, whenever there was a knock at the door, or when his mum returned from a shopping trip, he hoped for a split second that it was his dad coming back home. But so far, his wish hadn't been granted.

He'd asked his mum several times why his dad left, and more importantly, where he'd gone. But she would tell him she didn't know, or she would change the subject and not really answer him properly. She would always kiss and hug Oliver whenever he mentioned his dad, but she definitely didn't like talking about him.

There were several photos of his dad on top of the chest of drawers in Oliver's bedroom, but his mum took all the ones from the living room walls down, and packed them away. He presumed it upset her to look at them. He didn't understand why. Oliver missed his dad like crazy, but he always felt better whenever he looked at the photos. He'd also attempted a couple of drawings of his dad, but they didn't really look like him, a bit like his attempt at drawing Kaiser. Pictures of people and animals – in fact, all living things – never quite came out as he imagined. But still objects and scenery were very easy. Trees, gravestones, cars, tractors, hills, fields, houses, and even ghostly figures; they were all easy. People's faces and animals weren't his speciality. But that didn't mean he wouldn't keep trying.

3

It was now twelve-fifty. She'd been gone for an hour and thirty-seven minutes. She would usually have been back by now, but there was the odd occasion where she'd taken longer, presumably if she'd bumped into someone she knew and was chatting to them. He pushed aside the blinds and looked through the living room window. The long dirt track was empty. On a sunny day like today, when his mum or anyone else drove their car along the dusty, gravel road, the clouds of dust would hover in the air for a while, almost like smoke. But the air was clear.

Oliver went into his bedroom and sat at his desk once more. He took a fresh piece of paper from the top drawer, then picked up the charcoal pencil and thought about what to draw next. This was the most exciting time for him. He loved looking at a blank sheet, wondering what it could turn into. He loved the drawing process, but his heart always skipped a little as he looked at a new page. He could only imagine what story would be told by the time he'd finished the picture. There was something magical about taking a piece of paper and turning it into something that deserved to be taped to his bedroom wall.

Oliver also found numbers fascinating. Especially times. He would always try to work out how long something would take in his head. Counting the minutes of his mum's shopping trips were a regular thing. But he'd also work out to the minute how long he'd be asleep before the alarm clock at the side of his bed would wake him. He would do this before he went to bed, and after he'd woken up.

He'd gone to bed around nine-thirty the previous night, which was early for a Friday night, but his mum said she was tired and he should get an early night. He didn't understand why he had to go to bed early just because his mum was tired, but he didn't question her. Nine-thirty to seven-thirty was exactly ten hours, if he ignored being woken around six to the sound of the television in the living room.

Even at weekends he would set his alarm. He didn't want to waste time staying in bed. He wanted to get up and start the day so he could move onto his next drawing, or finish any half-done pictures.

His fascination with numbers would spread into his drawing hobby too.

He had three separate folders in his cupboard. One had a hundred pictures in it, one had a hundred and forty and the other had one hundred and eighty. His mum bought him a bigger folder each time he filled the last. With the three folders and the thirty-four pictures on the wall, that made a total of four hundred and fifty-four pictures... so far. He would cringe a little at the older pictures in the first folder, and the second wasn't much better. But he would never throw them away. They were his creations. And he also liked to see the quality of his drawing getting better as he drew more and more. Once his wall was full, he would ask his mum for another folder, maybe an even bigger one this time, and all the pictures from the wall would be put away, leaving the wall as another blank canvas, waiting for his new creations.

Oliver pushed his pencil into the pencil sharpener.

He knew his mum hated the noise it made; he didn't like the noise himself for that matter. His dad had brought it home from work, and apparently, there were quieter ones available, but Oliver liked this one. Maybe because his dad gave it to him, and he remembered watching him fix it to the desk with screws. Or maybe it was because it sharpened pencils to a very fine point, which was helpful when drawing fine lines. No other pencil sharpener had ever been as good, so he wanted to keep this one, regardless of the noise it made.

Before he could put pencil to paper, he heard a car in the distance.

He quickly jumped off his seat and ran as fast as he could through to the kitchen, then opened the tall cupboard next to the kitchen door, pushed the mop and broom to one side and climbed in before pulling the door closed on himself.

The previous week when his mum returned from her shopping trip, he'd hidden crouched down behind the door. He always enjoyed scaring her like that. She wasn't best pleased last week as she dropped a bag of shopping when he jumped out, grabbing her ankle as she walked in with the bags. But nothing was broken, so she eventually saw the funny side.

He waited quietly in the dark, hearing nothing but his own breathing, which was more rapid than usual as he felt the excitement of the game.

He waited.

He stood in the dark cupboard for a good couple of minutes. When nothing happened, he opened the door and poked his head out, listening for the sound of his mum's car. He couldn't hear any movement from outside of the bungalow. He couldn't hear anything at all.

Oliver climbed out of the cupboard, fighting with the falling mop handle as he pushed it back inside before closing the door, and walked back through to his bedroom to look through the window.

The car wasn't there.

He made his way to the living room and looked through that window. There was no car on the lane, but there was a cloud of dust hovering in the air. Oliver presumed it must've been a car from the farm.

He looked at the clock, did the maths in his head once more, and then shrugged and went back into his bedroom to begin his next masterpiece...

Available now in hardback, paperback, and eBook.

Printed in Great Britain
by Amazon